T0197616

The Gift of a Song

Seraphim D'Andrea

To order additional copies of this book, contact:
Xlibris
844-714-8691
www.Xlibris.com
Orders@Xlibris.com

Story and illustrations by Seraphim D'Andrea.
Author photograph by Amanda Reven.

The Gift of a Song created by Seraphim D'Andrea.
Published by
Nicholas D'Andrea, Jr.
dark horse studio
Waterbury, Connecticut

ISBN:	Softcover	978-1-4500-0682-8
	Hardcover	978-1-4500-0681-1
	EBook	978-1-6698-5945-1

Library of Congress Control Number: 2009912693

Print information available on the last page

Rev. date: 12/08/2022

This story is a dedication to my Mama, Papa, and all nine of my siblings. A special note of thanks to my brother Nick who inspired me to write this, and to my brother Daniel who always makes my blue days pink just by thinking of him!

I must take a moment to recognize my two angels here on earth. My Mama: From the days of afternoon kindergarten and how you put lipstick on me, to our trip to Jamaica and most importantly when you battled cancer and won! You are an inspiration and have been the greatest blessing God has given to me. You embody the true meaning of Mother and I thank you for this.

And to my other angel, also known as my hero: Thomas, you took a broken girl and made me whole again. If you never walked into that audience, I would not be here. You have loved me, supported me, and cared for me through some of the toughest battles for over eight years. Whenever I stumble, you catch my fall. "Thank you" is inadequate for all you have done to better my life, so to show my gratitude, I dedicate to you, "The Gift of a Song."

For those who have lost their battle with cancer, and for their loved ones, please know that you are in my heart and prayers.

God holds you now, my Big Boy Baron (my dearly departed German shepherd - Baby number five).

My name is Christmas and this is my story of the gift of a song.

It all began one Halloween night, my Daddy's favorite holiday. Mommy, Daddy, our doggies, and I were getting into our costumes. Mommy always made extra costumes for me and Daddy because we would change our minds all the time. Mommy always says I am a tiny version of Daddy, so she made me and Daddy matching costumes. Daddy was the Ice King, I was the Ice Princess, and our two dachshunds (Bella and Zeke) were snowflakes.

I wiggled with excitement knowing that shortly we would be walking out the door to my school's Halloween Party. Then all of a sudden, my belly gurgled as I remembered I had entered the costume contest. Mommy looked over at me, as she knew without my saying a word that I was scared.

She walked over and sang to me, "Have no fear, my little one . . . ," and the song went on from there. My belly calmed and my heart became happy. Mommy had a song for everything, and we would all sing along with her. Even the doggies would howl, but between you and me, they sounded better than Daddy. I mostly liked to listen to Mommy. Her voice was like an angel, and an angel is what Mommy was dressed as for Halloween.

The Ice King, Ice Princess, snow angel, and two snowflakes headed out the door. We had a great time dancing, eating more candy than our bellies could hold, and spooking ourselves as we went through the haunted house over and over again.

The announcement was made, "Hush, everyone! And the winner for the most unique costumes goes to . . . Christmas!" I won the prize. It was a candy apple the size of my head. Mommy was so proud of me that she said I could eat my prize when we got home. Oh, I couldn't wait to get home. It was the best Halloween EVER! We all loaded into the car. Daddy was driving so slowly. "Daddy, Daddy, hurry! I get to eat my candy apple once we get home!" Finally we are at our house. Daddy jumped out of the car. Bella and Zeke followed. I looked down to pick up my apple and saw that Daddy had my apple. "I'm going to eat this delicious apple," he said.

   "I'll get you, Daddy!" I exclaimed as I ran up the front steps and into the house to tickle him until the apple fell. We laughed so hard that we had forgotten about the apple, and just had a "tickle attack." Then, out of nowhere, we heard a loud noise on the front porch.

We ran out to see what it could be. "Mommy!" She was lying on the front steps. I looked at Daddy as he ran over to pick up Mommy. I had never seen that expression on Daddy's face before, and it scared me. Daddy picked up Mommy the way he carries me, and we got back into the car.

This time Daddy didn't drive slowly at all. I didn't speak a word. I didn't understand. Did Mommy eat too much candy? What could I say? All I could do is look at Mommy. We walked through a big door. Daddy said, "Christmas, I have to go with Mommy. We love you. Wait here like a good little girl. Daddy will be out soon." I sat alone, scared, until I saw a familiar face peak from behind a cocoa machine. It was Grandma! "Oh, Grandma!" She took me in her arms just like Mommy does, and began to sing to me as she held me tight. I felt less scared.

I started to fall asleep on Grandma's shoulder. I fought to keep my eyes from closing but as Mommy says, "sleepy time girl, close them eyes," so I did. I woke up and the sun was shining into the waiting room. I jumped up. "Mommy . . . where's my Mommy?" Grandma said that Mommy wanted to see me. Just Mommy and Christmas alone time - yay! I ran into her room. My Aunties and Uncles and Daddy were all there. Everyone looked sad, but why? She probably just has a belly ache from all the candy she had eaten, I thought. "Can everyone please step out for a minute so my lil' Christmas and I can have some Mommy time?" she asked.

I had missed Mommy all night! I get her all to myself! I climbed up onto Mommy's bed and laid my head on her chest like I always do, but something was different. I couldn't figure it out. "Mommy, did you get in trouble by the doctor for eating all that candy? If you did, then just tell him it was really me."

"No, my little one. Mommy is sick," she said. So I asked, "When will you get better?" Then Mommy sang me a song. "Little one, father God wants to bring your Mommy home to sit beside him in heaven to sing with the choir of angels. Be not afraid, for Mommy will no longer feel pain nor be sick."

I looked up at Mommy and cried. "Can I go and sing with you?"

"Well, sweet one, Daddy and the doggies need you here on earth to sing to them whenever they are sad. And then I can look down upon you and sing along. For remember, there is no greater gift than the gift of a song."

November came along with leaves of bright orange and red. Our house was full of my aunts and uncles, Grandma and Grandpa. Yummy turkey and all the fixin's. Pies and cookies were spread along the counter, just like Mommy liked. Mommy loved Thanksgiving mostly because that meant Christmas was just around the corner. Christmas was Mommy's favorite holiday.

Tradition was to go into the woods. Mommy, Daddy, and the doggies and I would cut down our own Christmas tree once we had rested a little while after our Thanksgiving feast. But Mommy was too weak, so all of my aunts and uncles, Grandma and Grandpa, and the puppies and I gathered our warm clothes and walked into the woods.

There stood the fattest Christmas tree I knew Mommy would love. "That's it, right there!" I exclaimed. With Daddy on one side and Grandpa on the other, they sawed through it. "Timber!" we all yelled as it fell to the ground. We brought our tree inside. Mommy's eyes lit up, just as I knew they would.

With challenged breaths, Mommy began to sing, "Oh, Christmas Tree." We all joined in singing along while putting ornaments on the tree.

November quickly moved into December. Snow fell each day. Mommy, Daddy, and I bundled up to make snow lanterns before the bus came to get me for school. I never wanted to leave mommy, for fear that she might not be there when I return. I was afraid that Father God would need Mommy to be with him so that she could sing with the angels on Christmas Day. She promised me that she would be there when I got home.

I sat in my class trying to figure out the greatest Christmas gift I could give Mommy when our principal made an announcement over the loudspeaker: "If anyone is interested in singing a solo for our Christmas concert, please go to the music room at 11:30." My heart leapt from my chest. Mommy always said that the greatest gift is the gift of a song.

I practiced everyday while I built snowmen, on the bus ride to school, and on the way home. Even in the bathtub. It had to be perfect for Mommy.

The night of the Christmas concert was here. Mommy was not feeling well that day but she would never miss a Christmas concert. I sat on her bed as she placed a scarlet ribbon in my hair. Daddy took Mommy by her hand, helping her to walk as we entered the auditorium. All my classmates and their parents were there, but I was not scared. My song was for Mommy and Father God to hear.

The lights dimmed as our chorus group took to the stage. Song after song, we sang as a group. Soon it would be my time to sing my solo. I could not wait!

"Next, we have a special treat for you all." I walked up to the center of the stage. I started to get nervous but then I just looked at my Mommy and saw her smile. I spoke into the microphone, "this is my Christmas gift to my Mommy... Silent Night."

I never took my eyes from her. As I sang the third verse, I saw Mommy's eyes close, and there stood a man made of light taking her by the hand. I continued to sing as the auditorium was filled with another voice singing with me, and there stood Mommy singing along - standing up tall, singing so strong. Father God, let me share with my Mommy one last time...the gift of a song.

Reverend Seraphim Ann Veronica D'Andrea resides in Lebanon, New Hampshire with the Loves of her life - her boyfriend and four dogs, more often referred to as her "babies." She is the ninth of ten talented children (six sisters and three brothers). A theatrical performer turned Reverend in 2004, she established a ministry, "On Angels Wings," serving New England with Christian services and counseling.

As a breast cancer survivor diagnosed in her early twenties (a rarity), she realized she wanted to combine her love of singing and Christmas, which lead to this timeless tale that touches upon a subject she knows well. She hopes this story will help those touched by illness, tragedy, and death by inspiring them to live life to the fullest - keeping hope in times of despair and having faith in miracles.

Printed in the United States
by Baker & Taylor Publisher Services